D0869354

Saint George
and the Dragon

Story by Diane DeFord

Illustrations by Edward Mooney

Dominie Press, Inc.

This is the tale of Saint George, a noble knight indeed. He fought a most ferocious dragon far away in the land north of Africa.

The dragon was enormous, a beast with long, slashing talons and strong wings. It was, by reputation, a most terrifying beast. It had spikes as sharp as knife blades down its long back. Its scales were as tough as armor. And it had an appetite large enough for several dragons.

Long ago, in the city of Silene, the most fearsome dragon ever known roared its command.

"Bring me your sheep and feed me well, or I shall make your city's wall a pile of broken stones!" it shouted.

The people ran to do the dragon's will, fear giving speed to their feet. They hugged each other as they watched it fly aloft, several sheep dangling from its enormous claws. And their fear increased as day after day, the dragon landed outside the gates of the city, demanding more sheep—until there were none left.

"What do you mean, you have no more sheep?" the dragon howled. Its roar was deafening. It reared up high and beat its wings hard upon the air. The people cowered as stones showered down from the top of the city wall.

"Then who among you will come forward, a man strong and brave to sate my hunger?" said the dragon.

With cries of protest, a single man was pushed forward. "I will go," he croaked. "But when will you leave this place?"

"Never!" shouted the dragon. "You've fed me well, but I want more!"

Then it leaped into the air and flew into the distance to watch the people in the city.

Stop here. Read the rest of the story silently.

The people ran to the king. They pleaded with him to save the men of their city. He met the dragon at the city gates and tried to barter for his people's lives. But alas, each day the dragon came, and each day another man was sacrificed to the dragon's monstrous appetite.

Finally, there were no men left in the city. The king went before the dragon. "You've eaten all our sheep, and you've eaten all our brave men," he said.

"Do you think I care if I eat your sheep, your men, or your maidens?" the dragon roared. "They are all the same to me!" It laughed as one of its claws swept into the crowd and grabbed a maiden away. As it rose into the air, the dragon shouted one last message.

"Tomorrow, I want your sweet daughter, you who are called king."

The next morning, the people crowded around a tree. The king cried as he tied his only daughter to the tree. "My dear, I have no choice," he said. "Maybe the dragon will leave us alone. We can but try."

Someone shouted, "Your majesty, look, a rider appears."

With that, a knight in shining armor brought his proud horse to a stop. "I've heard of your plight," he said. "You've been brave to stand up to such a frightful beast. But take heart, as I shall defeat him this very day."

Out of the sky, the sound of the dragon's powerful wings came closer. Finally, it landed on the ground. The knight, whose name was Saint George, yelled to the people, "Run to safety." They ran. Then he hoisted the king onto his faithful steed.

"I will bring your daughter back safely," Saint George said. "This is my vow."

The knight and the king rode back through the gates of the city together.

Saint George cut the ropes that held the maiden to the tree. He stood before her, glaring at the dragon.

"I am a much bigger meal for that stomach of yours," he cried. "My life for hers."

"That will suit me just as well!" said the dragon. "I can dream yet another night of the sweet meal she will make!"

The mighty beast breathed fire and lunged. But Saint George lunged, too, and his sword entered the soft flesh under the dragon's wing.

Good to his word, the noble knight slew the terrible dragon. Saint George became the patron saint of England for his noble deed.

Publisher: Raymond Yuen
Consultant: Adria F. Klein
Editor: Bob Rowland
Designer: Natalie Chupil
Illustrator: Edward Mooney

Published by:

ⓓ Dominie Press, Inc.

1949 Kellogg Avenue
Carlsbad, California 92008 USA

www.dominie.com

ISBN 0-7685-0653-0

Printed in Singapore by PH Productions Pte Ltd

4 5 6 7 8 9 10 11 PH 07 06 05 04 03